Madame Martine

SARAH S. BRANNEN

ALBERT WHITMAN & COMPANY
CHICAGO, ILLINOIS

FOR DREW

Library of Congress Cataloging-in-Publication data
is on file with the publisher.

Text and pictures copyright © 2014 Sarah S. Brannen
Published in 2014 by Albert Whitman & Company
ISBN 978-0-8075-4905-6

Printed in China.
10 9 8 7 6 5 4 3 2 1 BP 18 17 16 15 14

The design is by Jenna Stempel.

For more information about Albert Whitman & Company,
visit our web site at www.albertwhitman.com.

Madame Martine lived alone in a little apartment in Paris. She took the same walk every day. She shopped at the same stores. She wore the same coat. That was how she liked it.

Madame Martine lived near the Eiffel Tower, but she had never climbed it.

"Eh. It's a tourist thing," said Madame Martine.

Every morning
Madame Martine went
to Rue Cler and bought
chicken on Monday, scallops
on Tuesday, mushrooms
on Wednesday, beef on
Thursday, and fish on
Friday. On Saturdays she
fed the birds. On Sundays
she stayed home.

One rainy Saturday, Madame Martine saw a bright pair of eyes twinkling in a bush. The eyes belonged to a very small, very wet, very dirty dog.

Madame Martine looked up the street and down the sidewalk. No one seemed to be missing a dog. She reached down and a small tongue licked her hand.

It needs me, thought Madame Martine.

The dog looked at her and wagged its tail.

A dog might be nice, thought Madame Martine.

Madame Martine made up her mind. She tucked the dog under her arm and carried it home.

She washed it and toweled it dry. She shared her dinner.

"I think I'll call you Max," said Madame Martine.

In the morning, Madame Martine bought a croissant for breakfast. She also bought a collar, a leash, dog food, and a bowl for Max.

Madame Martine took Max shopping with her.

Two tourists asked Madame Martine the way to the Eiffel Tower, and she pointed up the street.

"It's beautiful!" they said. "What's it like at the top?"

"I don't know," said Madame Martine.

The tourists were surprised.

"Such a waste of time," said Madame Martine. "Climbing all that way up just to climb down again."

The tourists rushed away.

Max wagged his tail.

One ordinary Saturday, Madame Martine and Max walked under the tower on their way home. A squirrel dashed in front of them. Max leaped after it and jerked his leash out of Madame Martine's hand.

"Max!" cried Madame Martine.

Max raced up the stairs and under the turnstile.

"Stop!" called the guard. "No dogs allowed!"

"*Ma parole!*" said Madame Martine. She quickly bought a ticket and went in. Max was bounding up the stairs above her.

Madame Martine climbed after him. One flight, two flights, three flights.

"Max!" she called. Four flights, five flights, six flights. She stopped to catch her breath.

Max saw her resting and also stopped to catch his breath.

"*Alors*," muttered Madame Martine, starting up again. Max raced higher. The flight of stairs ended. First level.

Madame Martine's knees were shaking. She couldn't
see Max anywhere. A few tourists roamed the platform,
watching the sun set over Paris.

"*Maman!*" called a small boy. "There's a dog up there!"

Madame Martine saw Max climbing up to the second
level. She groaned and started up after him. So high! So windy!
Madame Martine gripped the rail and kept going.

As they reached the second level, the elevator to the top of the tower arrived. A few tourists got off. Max got on. Madame Martine ran to the elevator and made it on just as the doors closed.

She picked Max up. "Bad dog," she said.

Max licked her face.

Madame Martine closed her eyes and breathed deeply as the elevator creaked upward. It stopped and the doors opened.

"Oh!" said Madame Martine. "I never knew how beautiful it was."

"How did you bring that dog up here?" asked a guard. "Dogs are strictly forbidden."

"I didn't bring him up here," said Madame Martine. "He brought me."

Madame Martine and Max took the same walk every day. They wore the same coat. They sat in the same café. Then they went to Rue Cler and bought chicken on Monday, scallops on Tuesday, mushrooms on Wednesday, beef on Thursday, and fish on Friday.

Every Saturday they tried something new.

That was how they liked it.